THIS BO~
DATE ~

ACUP

22. N~
18. JUL

CW00969617

LANCASHIRE LIBRARY
WITHDRAWN FROM CIRCULATION

JONATHAN'S GHOST
SPITFIRE SUMMER

A Red Fox Book

Published by Random Century Children's Books
20 Vauxhall Bridge Road, London SW1V 2SA

A division of the Random Century Group

London Melbourne Sydney Auckland
Johannesburg and agencies throughout the world

First published by Piccadilly Press Ltd. 1989

Red Fox edition 1991

Text © Terrance Dicks 1989
Illustrations © Adriano Gon 1989

The right of Terrance Dicks and Adriano Gon to be
identified as the author and illustrator of this work
respectively has been asserted by them in accordance
with the Copyright, Designs and Patents Act, 1988.

This book is sold subject to the condition that it shall not,
by way of trade or otherwise, be lent, resold, hired out,
or otherwise circulated without the publisher's prior
consent in any form of binding or cover other than that in
which it is published and without a similar condition
including this condition being imposed on the subsequent
purchaser.

Printed and Bound in Great Britain by
Cox & Wyman Ltd, Reading

ISBN 0 09 968850 6

ROSSENDALE
LIBRARIES

Spitfire Summer

by

Terrance Dicks

Illustrated by Adriano Gon

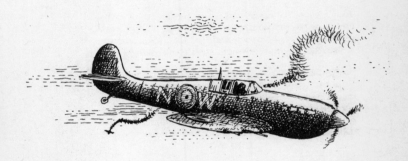

RED FOX

ROSSENDALE
LIBRARIES

DR	DB	DC	DE	DH	DS	DX	DW	OT	W
	✓								

04856480

CHAPTER ONE

Dogfight

The two fighter planes wheeled and whirled and swooped about one another in the bright blue summer sky.

One bore red, white and blue circles on the wings, the other the crooked black cross of the Nazi Swastika. British and German, Spitfire and Messerschmidt . . .

Suddenly the British plane seemed to gain the advantage. Swooping dangerously close to its opponent, the Spitfire looped first under then high above it, then swooped down out of the sun, machine-guns blazing. Smoke pouring from its fuselage, the Messerschmidt went into a spin, spiralling down towards the ground.

But the Spitfire had not escaped un-harmed. A thin spiral of smoke was coming from one wing and the engine had an erratic staccato note. Slowly the wounded Spitfire limped across the sky, struggling desperately to recover the safety of its home base . . .

Jonathan awoke sweating, his heart pounding furiously. For a moment he stared dazedly at the blue sky outside his bedroom window, as if somehow he was still out there with the duelling planes. He sat up on one elbow, rubbing his eyes, coming slowly back into the real world, realising it had only been a dream.

His alarm went off with a clatter and he reached out and switched it off.

His mother's voice came floating up the stairs. "Are you awake, Jonathan? You don't want to miss your train."

Jonathan grinned. Good old Mum, he thought. Instant hassle the minute you got your eyes open. "On my way, Mum," he yelled and jumped out of bed.

After a hasty wash at the handbasin in the corner of his room, Jonathan scrambled into his clothes. His rucksack, already packed,

was in the corner by the door. Shoving his toilet things into their waterproof bag, Jonathan jammed it into the rucksack and did up the straps. "Jonathan!" came his mother's voice again.

"Coming, Mum," yelled Jonathan. But instead of leaving he paused and looked round the room. "Well, this is it," he said cheerfully, addressing the empty air. "Soon as I've had my toast, Mum'll drive me to the station."

3

There was no reply. The empty room stayed empty. "Be good while I'm away," he said. "No getting up to mischief and scaring the neighbours."

Still nothing. "Oh, come on Dave, stop sulking," said Jonathan. "I know it's a bit rough on you my going away by myself, but there's weeks of the summer holidays to go yet and I'm going crazy stuck here at home. Great-Aunt Caroline's invitation was a life-saver. She even sent me the train ticket . . . "

Still there was no reply.

Jonathan shrugged. "All right, then, suit yourself. If you don't want to say goodbye, then don't. See you in a fortnight."

As Jonathan picked up his rucksack and turned towards the door he caught a flicker of movement in the corner of his eye. He turned and saw a shape appear, materialising on the end of his bed.

It was the form of a boy of about his own age, wearing shorts, grey socks wrinkled down around the ankles, grimy white tennis shoes and an open-necked cricket shirt. The boy's hair was cropped in a forties short-back-and-sides, his normally cheerful face was set

4

in an evil scowl. His name was Dave, and he was Jonathan's best friend. He was also a ghost, killed when a bomb hit this very same house in the war.

"Ah, so there you are," said Jonathan cheerfully. "I knew you wouldn't let me go without saying goodbye."

Dave still didn't speak. Instead, he twisted his face into an even more hideous scowl, stuck out his tongue, then put the thumb of his outstretched hand to his nose and wawggled the fingers in the traditional gesture of insult. Still in this same position, he faded slowly away.

Jonathan sighed, and carried his rucksack downstairs. Sometimes it wasn't easy being friends with a ghost.

Over the toast and marmalade, his mother sounded both puzzled and pleased at the same time. "It's very nice of your Great-Aunt Caroline to ask you to stay with her, but it's a bit strange as well."

"Strange how?" asked Jonathan through a mouthful of toast. "She must have heard how amazingly lovable I am."

His mother gave him a doubting look. "Well, maybe. The thing is, she's never wanted to have very much to do with the rest of the family before this."

"Maybe she's thinking of making me the heir to the family fortune," said Jonathan hopefully.

"That's just it, there isn't one. She lives in this big old house in the country all by herself. She's too poor to keep it up properly and too obstinate to sell it."

"Any other relatives about?"

"I don't think so. There was a nephew, a bit of a bad lot, but he got killed in the war I think, or maybe just disappeared. There was

6

something odd about it all. Some kind of family scandal that got hushed up." Jonathan's mother gave him a worried look. "If she is thinking about making you her heir, mind you don't go doing anything to spoil it. And watch your manners, Great-Aunt Caroline's one of the old school."

Jonathan looked at his watch. "Well, she won't be very impressed if I miss my train then, will she? We'd better get a move on."

* * *

Jonathan's mother had a busy day ahead of her, so she just dropped him off at the station, telling him at least three times not to get on the wrong train. Jonathan found the right train without too much trouble.

Choosing an empty carriage, he put his rucksack in the luggage rack, installed himself in a corner seat facing the engine and sat back, enjoying the luxury of his surroundings.

He wasn't left in peace for very long.

Two prosperous-looking, plump, red-faced young men, loaded down with umbrellas,

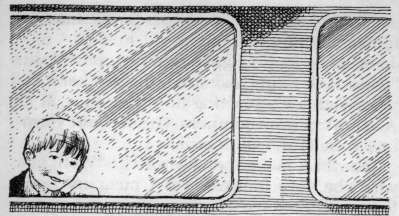

suitcases, briefcases and copies of all the more serious-looking newspapers, burst into the compartment and sat down, spreading themselves and their possessions over most of the seats, and talking all the time in loud voices. "So I said to J.B.," one of them bellowed, "J.B., I said, fifty million is definitely the bottom line. Well, he saw right away I meant business and climbed down at once . . ."

Jonathan gave a sort of internal groan and decided to go and look for somewhere quieter.

He was just about to stand up and get his rucksack when he realised that the older of the two men was glaring at him disapprovingly.

"I say, little boy, you're in First Class. Off you go now!"

Jonathan sat tight. He wouldn't have moved now for the world. He just sat and stared out of the window.

The train gave a sudden jolt and began drawing slowly out of the station.

The man leaned forward. "Did you hear me, boy? This is a First Class compartment."

Jonathan turned to look at him. "I'm perfectly well aware of that, thank you," he said politely.

"Now look here, I don't want any cheek. This is a First Class compartment and you need a First Class ticket to travel in it."

"Yes, I know that too, thank you."

By now the man was losing patience. "Have you got a First Class ticket?" he shouted.

Now Jonathan wasn't normally rude to strange adults, or to anyone else for that matter. Generally speaking he was a good-natured and fairly polite sort of boy. But if there was one thing that really made him mad it was the sort of grown-up who felt politeness was a one way street, that they

9

could be as rude as they liked, but still expected kids to treat them with respect. Now the second man joined in. He spoke slowly, loudly and very distinctly, the way some people speak to children or foreigners. "Do you have a First Class ticket?"

Jonathan leaned forward and spoke with equal clarity. "Are you a ticket collector, then? Because if you're not, I really don't see that it's any of your business."

The man began spluttering with rage. "Cheeky little oik. I've a good mind to throw you out myself."

He lunged forward, reaching for Jonathan's collar.

But somehow things went wrong.

His feet seemed to slide from under him, and he landed on the floor of the compartment.

His friend reached out to help him, but somehow he tripped up too, falling heavily on top of the man he was trying to help.

The two men thrashed about wildly, trying to extricate themselves from the narrow space and get up. Somehow the more they struggled the worse things became.

Their briefcases burst open, filling the air with important-looking papers. In his struggle to get free, one of the men caught his friend a painful clip over the ear, and moments later the second man's elbow connected with the end of his attacker's nose.

"Tickets please," said a new voice as the compartment door slid open. A tall, stern-faced ticket collector stood in the doorway, looking down in amazement at the two dusty, struggling figures on the floor. "Now then, what's going on here?"

"No idea," said Jonathan cheerfully. "These two came in shouting and then they seemed to get into a fight. I reckon they're drunk if you ask me."

The ticket collector helped the two men to disentangle themselves and get to their feet. They dusted themselves down, stuffing their papers back in their briefcases. Once they were more or less sorted out the older man said, "It's all this kid's fault. He's got no right to be in this compartment and he refused to show us his ticket."

"No reason why he should, sir," said the collector calmly. "That's my business not yours." He turned to Jonathan and said solemnly, "Tickets please!"

Equally solemnly, Jonathan produced his ticket and handed it over.

The ticket collector studied it, clipped it and handed it back. "All in order sir, thank you." Luckily Jonathan's unknown Great-Aunt Caroline had paid for him to travel in style.

He turned to the two men who had been watching all this in amazement.

"Tickets please."

12

Sulkily the two men began reaching for their wallets.

The wallets weren't there.

Frantically the two men searched all their pockets but with no success. The ticket collector was stony-faced. "If you don't have any tickets, gentlemen, I shall have to ask you to purchase them."

"How can we?" screamed the older man. "Our money's in our wallets with the tickets. Don't be such a fool."

"No need to be abusive, sir," said the collector stolidly. "I think you'd better come with me and see the Chief Guard."

"I bet that kid's got something to do with it," the older man began.

The younger man said, "Don't make matters worse, Freddy. We were only in here a few minutes and the kid didn't come anywhere near us. We must have had our pockets picked in that crowd, when we went through the barrier."

Protesting furiously, the older man let himself be led away.

When the compartment was empty again, Jonathan sat back and looked around.

"All right, Dave, I know you're around. Come out, wherever you are."

For a moment nothing happened. Then a voice came from above his head. "Wotcher, mate!"

Jonathan looked up. Hands behind his head, Dave lay stretched out on the luggage rack, using it like a hammock.

CHAPTER TWO

Haunted

"How did you know I was here?" asked Dave.

Jonathan sighed. "With all that chaos and confusion going on? Of course I knew you were here. Come on, hand 'em over!"

For a moment Dave looked blank. Then, "Oh, you mean these?" Two expensive looking wallets appeared in his hands. He chuckled. "Wonder what they'll do now? Maybe they'll have to work their passage, stoke the engine or something."

"Diesels don't need stoking," said Jonathan. "You'd better give those wallets back."

"What, and spoil all the fun?"

"You've already had your fun. I'm all in favour of teaching those twerps a lesson, but stealing's going too far. Anyway, one of them's already tried to accuse me. If those wallets are found here I'll be in real trouble. Go on, you give them back."

"All right, then, hang on," said Dave and vanished.

Jonathan sat staring at the outskirts of London as they flashed by the window. He had rather mixed feelings about Dave turning up. Dave's well-meant attempts at being helpful had caused Jonathan no end of trouble at school, and it looked as if very much the same thing might happen on this holiday.

Suddenly Dave reappeared, this time sitting on the seat beside him. "All taken care of. I put the wallets in their briefcases. They'll think they fell out in the struggle and got shoved in the cases by mistake. They're bound to find them sooner or later."

"Where are they now?"

"In the guard's van, having a hell of a row with the guard." Dave chuckled. "He still insisted they'd got to pay their fare, so they searched all their pockets and came up with a few crumpled notes and some change. In the end they managed to scrape up two fares between them. But this is the good bit. They didn't have enough for First Class, so they're going to have to go Second."

Jonathan burst out laughing. "Serve them right, they can see how the other half lives. Well, that takes care of them, now what about you?"

"How do you mean?"

"Well, what are you doing here?"

Dave looked hurt. "Aren't you glad to see me?"

"I suppose so," said Jonathan, and to be honest he was quite pleased. "But I thought you were tied to haunting the house? I mean, you can't haunt a train, can you?"

"Only if it's a ghost train," said Dave. He laughed at his own awful joke, then became serious again. "It's not only places that get haunted, it's people as well." He looked solemnly at Jonathan. "I, me old mate, am now haunting you. So, where you go, I go. Isn't that terrific?"

Jonathan sighed. "Terrific." He remembered, long ago, reading a ghost story called 'The Haunted Man.' Now, here he was, a haunted boy. It didn't have quite the same ring to it, but he supposed the principle was the same.

"Right then," said Dave cheerfully. "Now, where are we off to, and who's this old trout Great-Aunt Caroline?"

"She's my mother's aunt," said Jonathan. "From the posh side of the family, or at least, from the once-posh. Now she lives all alone in a big old house in Kent, right on the coast. So, at least we're going to the seaside."

"What, like Southend?" said Dave happily. "Cockles and whelks and candy-floss, rides on the scenic railway and boat trips round the harbour. Any more for the Skylark?"

"What?"

"That's what the boat man used to say, his boat was called the Skylark. When you were out at sea he stopped rowing and collected the fares. Anyone who couldn't pay had to swim back."

"I don't think this place is exactly Southend," said Jonathan. "I looked it up on the map. It's a tiny little place right out on the sea end of the Thames Estuary, miles from anywhere by the looks of it."

Dave sniffed. "Probably nothing there but sea and mud-flats."

"Apparently there used to be a big airfield there during the war," said Jonathan, trying to make the place sound a bit more interesting. "Spitfires used to fly out of it during the Battle of Britain."

Jonathan had a sudden quick flash of fighter planes circling in a blue sky, and suddenly he remembered his dream. He couldn't help feeling that the dream was very important, that his journey and the dream were somehow linked . . .

For a moment he sat staring out of the window. Then he shivered, and looked at his watch. "Anyway, we'll know before very long, it's not that long a journey really. We have to change at the end of the line and get some little local train . . . "

Despite Dave's arrival, the rest of the journey passed off without any more excitement. Jonathan ate the sandwiches his mother had insisted on providing, and got himself a coke from the buffet. On the way he caught sight of the two men from his compartment. They were sitting in a crowded Second Class compartment, surrounded by a jolly mum and dad with three lively, noisy children, all off to a day at the seaside. The littlest kid kept tipping one of the men's bowler hats over his eyes and roaring with laughter. The two men didn't look happy, but the kids were having a wonderful time.

*   *   *

Following the instructions in Great-Aunt Caroline's letter, they eventually changed from the big train, parting company with the jolly holiday-bound crowds and got onto a little local diesel.

The odd thing was that the two business-suited, bowler-hatted men changed with them.

They must have found the wallets, because Jonathan spotted them hurriedly buying tickets. However, the train was so small that it didn't even have a First Class carriage, and Jonathan took care to keep well away from them. This little train was nearly empty, so

20

he was able to sit and chat with Dave.

At the moment, Dave, quite real and solid to Jonathan but invisible to anyone else, was sitting opposite him in the empty carriage staring out of the window. He wasn't much impressed with what he was seeing, just flat green fields fringed by mud-flats and the misty sea in the distance.

"Looks like the end of the world to me.

What on earth are we going to do here?"

Jonathan shrugged. "Go for nice long walks, do a bit of bird watching."

"Terrific!"

"Look, you're not even supposed to be here, so for goodness sake lay low and keep out of mischief. Great-Aunt Caroline must be pretty ancient by now and I don't want you to scare her into popping off."

"Me, get into mischief?" said Dave looking hurt. "As if I would . . . "

They were drawing into a tiny station by now and Jonathan looked out of the window at the sign. "Marsh Halt. Come on, we're here!"

Grabbing his rucksack, Jonathan got off the little train.

Only two other people got off the train with him – the two businessmen he'd had trouble with earlier.

"I wonder what they're up to," said Jonathan. He turned to Dave, only to find that he'd disappeared.

The two men glared indignantly at Jonathan for a moment, then decided to pretend he didn't exist.

Jonathan did the same and they all walked off the platform determinedly not seeing each other.

Outside the little station there was nothing but an empty country lane. Jonathan stood looking round him helplessly. Not far away, the two businessmen were doing exactly the same thing, still pretending that he was invisible.

A little old man with a brown wrinkled face and a bald head with a fringe of white hair emerged from the tiny station and stood blinking at them in amazement. Probably the first time anyone has ever got off here, Jonathan thought.

One of the two men called, "I say, old chap, any chance of a taxi? We want to get to the local inn."

The old codger gave a sort of dry creaking sound which, Jonathan realised, must be a chuckle. "Pub be two moile down the road," he said, pointing. "And there ain't been no taxi here since nineteen fifty-three."

He turned and shuffled back into the station.

Suddenly a sort of rattling, chugging sound

came from the opposite direction to that in which he'd pointed and an extraordinary-looking vehicle came puttering around the bend of the lane. It was a huge open touring-car of the kind Jonathan associated with the twenties or thirties with a long bonnet, huge wheels and a very high body. It was the kind of car that really needed a chauffeur, but instead, there in the driving seat sat an equally extraordinary-looking old lady, very tall and thin with huge black eyes and an aristocratic looking beaky nose. She wore a long, flowing black dress.

The car juddered to a halt outside the station and stood shuddering, the engine still running. The old lady stared down at them, looking from the two men to Jonathan as if in puzzlement.

"I am looking for a young man called Jonathan Dent."

Jonathan stepped forward. "That's me."

The old lady looked at him as if he were something she'd ordered which didn't quite come up to standard. "I was expecting someone rather older."

Jonathan decided that if he was going to

24

spend a couple of weeks with this terrifying old bat, he'd better get things on the right footing from the start.

"I'm very sorry about my age," he said politely. "But I'm afraid there's not very much I can do about it."

The dark eyes flashed fiercely, and for a moment Jonathan wondered if he'd gone too far. Then the old lady smiled. "No, of course you can't," she said. "Do forgive me, you must think me very rude. I'm Caroline Boone, your great-aunt."

She held out her claw-like hand and Jonathan shook it. "How do you do, Great-Aunt Caroline?"

"Jump in," ordered the old lady briskly. "Put your luggage in the back and sit here beside me."

Jonathan obeyed.

The two businessmen had been watching this exchange in some astonishment. The younger of them stepped forward. "Miss Boone?"

The old lady looked down at him. "You have just heard me say so."

"Jack Potter, of Potter and Purbright. You

may remember we wrote to you."

"I am not in the habit of discussing my business affairs in the street, young man."

"I was wondering if we could come and see you."

"You may write to my lawyer for an appointment in the normal way. Now, if you will excuse me?"

Jack Potter seemed quite undeterred by his frosty reception. "I suppose you couldn't give us a lift to the inn could you? We're a bit stuck . . . "

'You suppose correctly," said the old lady acidly. "Unfortunately, I happen to be going in the opposite direction. The inn is only two miles down the road. By the look of you, the walk will do you good."

The car shot suddenly forwards, the old lady did a neat 'U' turn and rattled away.

As it rounded the bend, Jonathan turned and saw Potter and Purbright pick up their briefcases and suitcases and start trudging down the lane.

They looked tired already.

*　　*　　*

The old car put on a surprising turn of speed once it was moving, and it seemed to be going even faster in the narrow country lanes. Great-Aunt Caroline drove sitting bolt upright and glaring straight ahead, and somehow Jonathan knew that if anyone or anything appeared ahead, she would expect it to get out of her way. It probably would, too.

The speed and the noise made conversation difficult, and Jonathan guessed that the old lady probably disapproved of idle chatter. In addition she seemed to have something on her mind, and he heard her muttering something about "The vultures are gathering already."

He glanced back at the back seat to make sure his rucksack was okay, and saw Dave sitting beside it, clearly enjoying the ride. Dave winked and gave him a thumbs up sign, but to Jonathan's relief he made no attempt to speak.

The lane led them across flat green marshy fields with the sea beyond and eventually to the kind of old dark house in which Dracula would have felt quite at home. It managed to look sinister in the bright mid-day sunshine,

and Jonathan hated to think how it would look on a dark and stormy night.

Great-Aunt Caroline drove the car up the drive, past the front of the house, through an archway into a cobbled yard, and finally into an old stable, now obviously serving as a garage.

Grabbing his rucksack – by now Dave had disappeared again – Jonathan followed the old lady through a back door into a big old stone-flagged kitchen, where a meal of bread and cheese and salad was set out on the wooden table. Great-Aunt Caroline waved towards it. "For you, young man."

Jonathan sat down at the table. "What about you?"

"At my age I subsist largely on tea and toast. I shall endeavour to provide some sort of evening meal, though I warn you, cooking isn't really one of my talents."

Jonathan started eating and Great-Aunt Caroline made a pot of tea, using a kettle which was simmering on an old-fashioned coal-burning cooker. She eventually pecked at a little bread and cheese herself, but only when Jonathan said he'd had enough.

Suddenly Jonathan realised that in this household food was probably in short supply.

"Mum gave me some money to put towards my food," he said casually.

"Certainly not, I wouldn't hear of it."

"I'll find the local shops and lay something in then," said Jonathan calmly.

For a moment the old lady glared fiercely at him, then her lips twitched. "You seem to be a very obstinate young man."

"Must run in the family," said Jonathan cheerfully. He was beginning to warm to his Great-Aunt. She was the sort of person who couldn't help trying to dominate everyone she met, and despised the ones who let her get away with it. The trick was not to stand any nonsense.

Which brought him to his next point. Polishing off the last of his salad, he took a swig of his cup of tea and looked thoughtfully at his Great-Aunt.

"Thanks very much for the meal," he said politely. "Now maybe you'll tell me why you've asked me down here."

CHAPTER THREE

The Summoning

Great-Aunt Caroline gave him the full benefit of her haughty stare.

"I should have thought my reasons were obvious enough."

"Such as?" said Jonathan encouragingly.

"A desire to see something of my family again, the wish for a little younger company, the hope of providing some deserving child with a little innocent pleasure . . ."

Jonathan burst out laughing. "I'm sorry but I don't believe a word of it."

"Well, really!" Great-Aunt Caroline rose in fury. "I am not accustomed to being spoken to in that manner."

"I'm sorry, I didn't mean to sound rude. But it really won't do, you know."

"What will not do?"

"These reasons of yours. According to my mum, you've done very well without seeing the family for years, and I bet if it was up to you you'd keep it that way. And as for wanting young children and giving some deserving child innocent pleasure – well, firstly you don't seem the type who'd want kids around, secondly, you obviously thought I was a lot older than I really am when you asked me."

Slowly Great-Aunt Caroline sat down. "I see you are intelligent as well as obstinate. You're quite right of course, I've been less than frank with you." She paused for a moment. "As you say, I've managed happily on my own for quite some time now. But recently things have become – difficult. It's become harder and harder to keep the house up on the little money I have left and there have been pressures from outside."

"What pressures?"

"Those two men who were on the train with you, Mr Potter and Mr Purbright . . . They're

33

property developers of some kind and they want to buy some sea-front land I own and . . . develop it."

"Sounds like the answer to all your problems."

Great-Aunt Caroline shuddered. "And ruin the whole area? My family have lived in the village for generations, and I still feel I have a duty towards it."

Jonathan frowned. "I can see how you might feel you needed some help – but why me?"

Great-Aunt Caroline looked puzzled. "I don't know. I just woke up one morning with the conviction that you, and you alone, were the one I needed. I had some vague idea you were much older, a lawyer or an accountant or something, though where I got it from heaven knows."

"Weird," said Jonathan briefly. He remembered his feeling on the train, that his journey had a purpose and that it was linked to his dream. "Well, what happens now?"

"I must confess I usually have a little sleep in the afternoons, but I scarcely imagine that you . . ."

Jonathan shook his head. "Not since I was about three anyway. I'd like to take a look around. Trouble is, you seem to be a bit of a way from anywhere. Didn't I see an old bike in your garage?"

She nodded. "It belonged to my nephew. It's been standing there ever since he — went away. I'm not sure if it's still in working order, though I've always looked after it."

Jonathan got up. "I'll take a look. Don't worry, I can always hoof it if I have to."

* * *

35

But the bike, when Jonathan inspected it, was in surprisingly good condition, almost as if it had spent the years in some bicycle museum. It was an ancient model with heavy tyres and solid mudguards, sit-up-and-beg handlebars and a carrier. The tyres were flat, but when they were pumped up they stayed up, and very soon Jonathan was wobbling down the drive towards the lane.

Great-Aunt Caroline had given him directions, and even drawn him a rough map. Left at the end of the drive took you straight to the village, right to the sea wall and the sea. Jonathan had worked out that if he turned right and rode to the sea wall and then left when he reached it, he could ride around the coast to the village and then take the direct route from the village back home.

After the lightweight, aluminium frame, drop handlebars sports model Jonathan was used to back home, the old bike felt like a tank but it got him along and by pedalling hard he was even able to get up a fair bit of speed.

A familiar voice spoke in his ear. "This is a bit of all right, isn't it?"

Glancing over his shoulder, he saw Dave perched on the carrier behind him.

"You're coming down in the world," said Jonathan. "First you were haunting a house, then a train and now a bike."

"I'm haunting you mate, and don't you forget it,' said Dave. "Where are we off to anyway?"

Dave told him. "Weren't you around when I was in the kitchen?"

"No, I stayed outside. I don't like the feel of that house somehow. It's spooky.

Dave's presence on the bike didn't seem to make pedalling any harder – what did ghosts weigh after all, thought Jonathan – and the lane, like the fields around, was dead flat. Eventually they came to a brick wall almost hiding a cluster of weathered huts, topped by a rusty barbed-wire fence.

"That must be the old airfield," said Jonathan.

Dave leaped off the bike. "Right, let's go and take a look."

Leaning the bike against the wall, they walked into the airfield and stood looking around. They were in the middle of the little group of huts that had once been the airport buildings, and in the distance stretched the flat green fields that had once been the airstrip.

Suddenly Jonathan saw a group of young men sprawled outside the huts, some on deck-chairs, some on old wooden chairs dragged outside, others on the ground. Some of them wore flying suits and heavy sheepskin jackets, others were in their shirtsleeves. One of them looked up and stared hard at him.

"Looks as if the place isn't disused after all,"

38

said Jonathan. "Some local flying club must have taken it over. Surely they're in uniform, though . . ."

Dave didn't answer, and when Jonathan turned round, Dave wasn't even there . . .

Suddenly there was a whistling scream and one of the huts close to the edge of the field exploded in smoke and flame.

The roaring of engines filled the air and a loud voice crackled over the loudspeaker system. "Scramble, scramble, scramble! All pilots to their aircraft immediately. Airfield under attack!"

More bombs whistled down and the pilots leaped to their feet and began running towards the planes parked at intervals along the airfield.

Jonathan joined in the desperate stampede with the rest. He just had to get to his Spitfire and get airborne. A plane on the ground was a sitting target and squadrons had been destroyed that way. They were stretched desperately thin as it was, and couldn't afford to waste a single plane or a single pilot . . . Some fool was getting in his way, holding him back. A voice was calling, "Jonathan, Jonathan, come back . . ." The funny thing was, Jonathan wasn't even his name. He wished it was, better than a damn silly name like Tristram. Thank heaven none of the others knew the truth . . .

"Jonathan, come back, it's not safe," yelled the voice.

Jonathan felt a sort of mental tug, and suddenly he was standing in the middle of the quiet, deserted airfield, with Dave shaking him by the arm.

Jonathan stared dazedly at him. "What happened?"

"You tell me, mate. You just went away from me."

Jonathan told him what he'd seen and felt.

It was clear that Dave was badly shaken. "You went *back*," he whispered. "Back to their time, to the Battle of Britain. You mustn't do that, mate, it's too dangerous."

"I didn't exactly have much choice. I was suddenly *there*."

"You were summoned," said Dave solemnly. "Drawn there . . . Someone from the past *wants* you there . . . "

"Why did you say it was dangerous?"

"Because you were out of your body, weren't you? For a time, you were a ghost, like me."

"But my body was still alive, *here*. And I'm all right now."

"You're all right because you got back — because I called you back."

"Suppose I hadn't?" asked Jonathan. "Got back, I mean?"

"You'd have been stuck in that time forever."

"And what about the rest of me, that bit that was still here?"

"If you take the soul from a body, you're left with a sort of zombie. After a bit the body just withers and dies." Dave's voice was urgent. "Listen mate, if they try to pull you back there again, you've got to fight it."

"Hang on a minute," objected Jonathan. "You took me back to your own time once."

"You were dreaming, that time, and I was looking after you. This is different. Different, and dangerous . . ."

"I actually seemed to be someone else while it was happening," said Jonathan slowly. "Someone called Tristram."

Dave stared at him in horror. "You were possessed," he whispered. "Crikey, it's worse than I thought."

Jonathan shivered, suddenly cold in the blazing sun. "Let's get away from here."

They scrambled through the barbed wire and Jonathan heaved the old bike upright, and pedalled away from the airfield as fast as he could.

* * *

Some time later he was pedalling along the

43

path on top of the sea wall with water on both sides of him.

The water on his right was the sea and on his left was an enormous long, thin lake, a sort of lagoon. The whole coast was peaceful and deserted, and Jonathan found it hard to remember his recent terrifying experience. After all, midnight, not daylight was the time for ghosts. A phrase drifted into his mind, "The ghost in the mid-day sun . . . "

He turned to Dave who was back on the carrier. "What's going on then, Dave? Why me?"

"Search me, mate." Dave's voice was unusually serious. "That's what you've got to find out. I reckon that ghost, the other one I mean, wants something from you."

"But what?"

Dave shrugged. "Like I said, it wants something. And until you find out what it is and do it, it'll keep after you."

"Can't you help me?"

What was the use of having a resident ghost, thought Jonathan, if it couldn't help you out in a spot of bother with its fellow spooks?

Dave said, "I'll try. But it's dangerous, even for me."

"Why?"

"Look, I'm here because I want to be, right? But some ghosts are on earth because they *have* to be. They're tied to earth by some grudge, some piece of unfinished business. They spend years brooding on whatever's bothering them, and well, they can go a bit crazy. A really powerful one can just — wipe you out . . . "

They came to the turn-off that led down into the village.

There wasn't a lot to see in the village – a shop that sold everything you could ever possibly want, a garage and a pub, all grouped round a stagnant pond with a few dispirited ducks.

Jonathan visited the shop first, using the money his mother had given him to stock up with a variety of packets and cans and a few bottles as well. The results of his shopping filled up two large plastic bags which he lashed like saddlebags, one each side of the carrier on his bike.

The cycling and the shopping had made him thirsty, so he decided to explore the possibilities of the village pub.

Jonathan leaned his bike against the wall and went inside the cool dark bar. It was empty except for an old rustic in the corner sipping his pint, and a plump, motherly-looking lady behind the bar.

Before the lady could tell him he was too young to be in the pub Jonathan said, "Do you think I could have a coke or a lemonade or something? I'm dying of thirst."

"You can have a lemonade with pleasure, my love," said the landlady. "Only you'll have to drink it outside, 'cos of the licensing laws, see. You go and sit outside and I'll bring it, all right?"

Jonathan paid for his drink and went outside, sitting at one of the unoccupied tables.

The landlady came out with his lemonade. She looked at his bike. "Having a cycling holiday, my dear?"

"Well, not exactly," said Jonathan, grinning at the thought of touring on that iron monster. "I'm staying in the village for a bit — with my Great-Aunt Caroline, up at the house."

The landlady was impressed. "Well now, fancy that. She never has no company usually. Not like the old days. Once upon a time there was always people up at the big house but that's long gone." She rattled on a bit about the good old days when, apparently, the house had been the social centre of their countryside for miles around.

"Course, that's all finished now," she said sadly. "House parties and dances and shooting parties there was, so my mum used to tell me . . . "

"Were you here during the war?" asked Jonathan. "When there were fighters at the airfield?"

The landlady sighed. "That I was. Mind you I was only a little girl then. I used to help my mum collecting glasses, and washing up behind the bar."

Her eyes widened, as she stared back into the past. "We used to be crowded every night, then. Short life and a merry one the pilots used to say – and it was short enough for some of those poor boys. You know what they used to do?"

"No, what?"

"Well, they'd come in in little groups, like, little gangs of pals. And every now and again, you'd notice one of the group wasn't there any more. He was . . . missing. But the rest would all be quite cheerful – and they'd still buy the missing one a drink. They'd buy him his usual, and that drink would be just left there on the bar. And there it'd stay, all the evening, no-one would mention it, no-one would touch it. End of the evening they'd all pile into their old cars and roar back to the base. And a few nights later there was another one missing, another untouched drink on the bar . . . "

She smiled sadly. "Still, you don't want to hear all that, young lad like you. Terrible the way we old folk do go on about the war . . . "

"No, it's very interesting," said Jonathan. "Really, I mean it."

. . . And suddenly he was in a smoky, noisy bar, crowded with blue uniformed figures, laughing and chatting, and shouting orders for more drinks. Over in the corner a jolly group was singing.

Bless 'em all
Bless 'em all
The long and the short and the tall . . .

Jonathan was standing near the bar, but he wasn't one of the noisy, happy crowd. For some reason he was . . . apart.

A plump, pretty young woman was serving drinks, while from behind the bar a big-eyed, long-haired little girl surveyed the scene as she rinsed glasses in a sink.

A pilot officer with a ginger moustache was

buying a round of drinks.

"Five pints of bitter, a gin and tonic, and a brandy and soda."

He put the drinks on a battered tin tray, then added, "Oh yes, and another bitter for Tom." When the drinks arrived, the ginger-moustached pilot put the extra bitter carefully on the bar. Then looking straight at – no, straight through Jonathan he said, "Well, cheers Tom. There was no time to get to know

you, but you seemed like a pretty good type."
Raising a hand in farewell, he picked up the
tray and turned away.

Jonathan, though of course he wasn't
Jonathan any more, reached out a hand for
the drink — his drink. But his shadowy hand
passed right through the glass . . .

CHAPTER FOUR

The Deal

Somewhere far away, a voice was calling, "Jonathan! Come back, come back . . ."

He heard Dave's voice in his mind. "You've got to fight it . . . fight it . . . fight it . . ."

Jonathan made a mighty effort to remember not only where but who he was – and suddenly he was standing outside the pub in the hot sunshine with the landlady looking at him in concern.

"You all right, love? You looked miles away for a moment."

"I think I was," said Jonathan. "Or rather, years away."

The landlady looked baffled and Jonathan

said, "I'm all right, honestly, I just came over dizzy for a moment, must be the heat."

"It's my fault, keeping you out here chatting in the sun. Not often I get a chance to talk about the old days. No-one remembers, now, no-one wants to know. Just me and the old Wingco."

"Wingco?"

"The Wing Commander. He was here when the old field was still a fighter base, in the Battle of Britain. He liked the place so much he came back here to retire."

"I'd like to meet him," said Jonathan politely.

The landlady looked inside the pub at the clock over the bar. "He'll be here for his late lunchtime pint pretty soon. You'll see him if you hang on."

"Can't wait, I'm afraid, I've got to be getting back. Another day, maybe."

Jonathan was still feeling shaken and he was keen to get away. But it was too late.

A slim silver-haired old gentleman in a Royal Air Force blazer strode up to the pub.

"There you are, Wingco," said the landlady delightedly. "This young gentleman is interested in the old days, when the fighters were at the airfield."

"Is he indeed?" The old gentleman rubbed his hands. "Is he indeed? I'll have my usual pint, my dear, and if your young friend will join me in his usual tipple, I'll be glad to tell him all he wants to know."

Jonathan was trapped.

A few minutes later they were sitting at one of the tables, drinking beer and lemonade respectively.

"Right my lad," said the Wingco, after his first swig of beer. "We'll start with a bit of potted history. How much do you know about the Battle of Britain?"

"Not as much as I should, sir, I'm afraid."

The Wingco took another sip of beer. "Right! It's summer 1940 and Britain's losing the war. In fact Hitler says we've already lost and just haven't realised it yet. British Army's been defeated in France, what's left evacuated from Dunkirk."

"So things were looking pretty black?"

"Couldn't be blacker. Hitler's conquered France, Belgium, Holland. He's made himself the Master of Europe – except for us. Now, what's Hitler's next step?"

Jonathan jumped. "Er – invade England?"

"Exactly. Operation Sealion, plan to invade England all worked out – but . . . " The Wingco pointed seawards. "One major problem – out there."

That was an easy one. "The Channel," said Jonathan.

Next to Jonathan, though invisible to the Wingco, sat Dave listening in fascination to the story of events he'd lived through.

55

"Right," said the Wingco again. "Invasion by sea tricky business. German Navy, German Army, say can't be done unless –"This time he pointed upwards. Jonathan thought hard. "Unless Germany controlled the air?"

"Precisely." The Wingco seemed delighted at having found such a bright pupil. "Whereupon Goering . . . "

"He was the fat one wasn't he?" asked Jonathan.

"Exactly! Fat chap in a sky-blue uniform, in charge of the German Air Force. "Leave it to me, says fatty, my brave lads will drive the British from the skies."

At this point Dave blew a hearty raspberry.

The Wingco frowned, like someone who hears a distant noise. "Sorry, did you say something?"

"No, no," said Jonathan, scowling at Dave to shut up.

"Anyway," the Wingco went on, "that was the Battle of Britain. Went on right through the summer of 1940. They sent their fighters and bombers over day by day, we fought back

with everything we'd got. Short of planes, short of pilots, short of everything. One big advantage, Radar! We could usually see the blighters coming, put our planes where they were needed."

He took another swig of beer. "End of the day, we won, or at least, we didn't lose. Goering never got command of the air, Germany never invaded. Hitler keeps postponing Sealion, finally goes off the whole idea, and attacks Russia instead. Damnfool idea, probably lost him the war, that and the Yanks coming in on our side."

Suddenly a voice interrupted them "I say, have you got a minute?" A young man in grey flannels and an open-necked shirt was standing in the pub doorway.

For a moment Jonathan didn't recognise him. Then he saw it was one of the two businessmen he'd met on the train. He looked a lot less stuffy in his casual gear, and his manner was a good deal more friendly.

"I'd very much like us to have a little chat if you could spare me a moment." The request was made so charmingly it was impossible to refuse, and besides, Jonathan was curious as to what was behind it.

"Okay," he said obligingly. He turned to the Wingco, "Goodbye sir."

The young man said, "Jolly good, let's have a drink on it, shall we? What'll you have?"

"How about a Vodka Martini, shaken and not stirred?" The young man gaped and Jonathan said hurriedly, "Sorry, too many James Bond movies, another lemonade will do fine."

"Splendid. A dry sherry for me and a lemonade for my friend."

When they were sitting at another of the

outside tables with their drinks the young man held out his hand. "Jack Potter, of Potter and Purbright. You met my partner, old Freddie. Bit of a twit, to be honest, but loads of contacts."

Jonathan shook hands. "Jonathan Dent."

"I'm afraid we got off on the wrong foot rather, earlier on. Apologies and all that." Jack Potter grinned. "To be honest, if we'd known who you were, we'd have treated you with a lot more respect. Your Great-Aunt is very important to us right now."

"Why?" asked Jonathan bluntly.

"Freddy and I are developers in a small way, just starting up on our own. We've got this really splendid scheme for a marina. This is the deal . . . "

*   *   *

"So what's a marina?" asked Dave, now back on the carrier as Jonathan cycled home.

"Sort of a specially built harbour for small boats, pleasure yachts and that sort of thing. Boating's very big these days."

Dave said wonderingly, "Yachts! In my day

most people didn't even have cars."

"Anyway," said Jonathan, "these two characters have got it all worked out but they can't start without a strip of sea-front land Great-Aunt Caroline owns, just by that lagoon we saw."

"And she won't sell to them?"

"She won't even talk to them. She reckons it goes against her obligations to the village or something."

"So where do you come in?"

"I said I'd try and get her at least to listen to them . . . though whether she'll listen to me . . . "

Great-Aunt Caroline was up and pottering around the garden when Jonathan got back, and since she seemed quite happily occupied, Jonathan spent the afternoon exploring, first the huge rambling garden, and then the big old house. There were scores of rooms, most of them unused. The one he was to sleep in had a four-poster bed, velvet curtains and lots of heavy oak furniture. Jonathan was afraid it would be like sleeping in a museum.

"A house like this is really worth haunting," said Dave, materialising suddenly and bouncing on the bed. "None of your modern rubbish."

"Why not take it over?"

Suddenly serious, Dave said, "Because there's someone here already."

"Another ghost, you mean?"

Dave nodded. "I could feel it the minute we came in."

"What sort of a ghost?" asked Jonathan, a little nervously. "A friendly one, like you?"

Dave shook his head. "I doubt it, somehow.

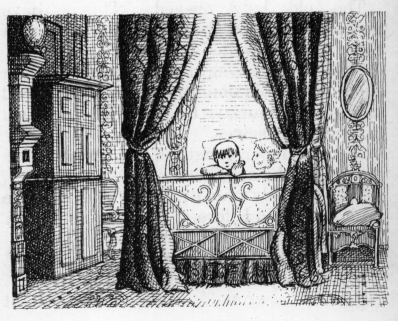

I'm doing my best to track it down . . . "

And with that he vanished.

*   *   *

When Great-Aunt Caroline came in from the garden, she found Jonathan in the kitchen preparing supper.

"Sausages, eggs and chips," he said, "basic but nourishing. Just you sit down and leave it all to me."

The old lady obeyed. "Things have certainly changed. In my days, young men expected to be waited on."

"You'd wait a long time to be waited on in our house," said Jonathan. "Mum works all kinds of odd hours, so Dad and I have learned to cope by ourselves."

During supper, Jonathan told her about his meeting with Jack Potter.

The old lady shuddered. "Vultures!" she said. "As I said before, it goes against all my sense of obligation to the village."

"You know," said Jonathan thoughtfully, "I'm not so sure you haven't got it all wrong."

"Got it wrong!" hissed Great-Aunt

62

Caroline, looking as if she was about to turn him into a toadstool any minute.

Jonathan nodded. "I mean, in the good old days, this house must have meant a lot in the life of the village. Jobs for servants and gardeners and gamekeepers and heaven knows what, money spent on food for all those house parties . . . "

"Go on."

"Well, what can you do for them now?"

"Nothing," said the old lady bitterly. "Death and taxes have reduced me to a state where I can hardly look after myself, let alone help others."

"This marina," said Jonathan. "It would mean lots of jobs when it was being built, lots of jobs when it was going too. Boat building and repair, work on engines, sail-making, not to mention jobs in the yacht club that goes with it. It could bring the village back to life."

"I will not have the whole village ruined," said the old lady furiously.

"Who's talking about ruining it? Nice little harbour with yachts in it, a few well-designed buildings. You could be on the Board of Directors, keep them all in order . . . "

But it was no use. Great-Aunt Caroline refused to even think about the marina proposition, and wouldn't even consider meeting Potter and Purbright.

Jonathan decided to leave it at that. He had no particular reason to do Potter and Purbright any favours, though he genuinely thought the proposed marina could be a very good thing, both for the village and for Great-Aunt Caroline herself. Not only would it provide her with some much needed income, it would give her something new to think about. Jonathan had already realised that she spent much of her time brooding over the tragedies of the past.

After supper she picked up the big oil lamp and led Jonathan along gloomy corridors to the portrait gallery.

The shadows of the old house seemed to press in on the flickering lamp.

"Did you ever think about putting in electricity?" asked Jonathan.

"Oh yes, we were pioneers. We used to have our own generator. Unfortunately it broke down years ago, and I can't afford to have it repaired."

In the portrait gallery, family portraits sprang out of the darkness. Men in armour, men in doublet and hose, bewhiskered dignitaries in the colourful uniforms and sober frock-coats of the Victorian age . . .

The old lady lingered longest on the uniformed portraits at the far end of the long gallery, and Jonathan realised that these were people she had actually known. "My father and all my uncles were lost in the First World War. I lost my three brothers and the man I was going to marry in World War Two."

Jonathan didn't know what to say. "They must have been very brave."

"They were heroes," said the old lady bitterly. "They were heroes and now they are dead. Be thankful you won't have to give your life for a patch of African desert or a few yards of trampled French mud."

"Yes, it's different now," said Jonathan. "We'll all go together when we go."

He pointed to a blank space at the end of the line of portraits. "There seems to be room for just one more."

"That space was intended for my nephew, the only male survivor on my side of the family. But his portrait will never hang there."

"Why not?"

The old lady was silent for a moment. Then she said, "He was always wild and reckless. What they used to call a rake, always in trouble, drink, women, gambling. He had great charm though, and usually managed to talk his way out of trouble. Many a time I paid his debts, gave him a fresh start."

"So what happened to him?"

"We quarrelled bitterly at the beginning of

the war. He refused to join up, said he didn't want to join the long line of dead heroes. I told him he was a disgrace to the family, gave him money for the last time and he went away. I never saw him again. I heard he'd gone to Canada, and on to America — they were neutral then."

Suddenly Jonathan's dream flooded back into his mind. "Was his name Tristram?"

A gust of wind rushed through the gallery, slamming a loose shutter against the wall and almost blowing out the oil lamp.

The old lady shielded it with her hand. She stared at Jonathan in amazement.

"That's right . . . But how could you know that? My nephew's name was Tristram . . . Tristram Boone."

*   *   *

That night Jonathan lay awake in the big four-poster, looking at the flickering candle that he didn't quite like to blow out.

Suddenly Dave appeared on the end of the bed. "You ought to get out of here, mate, soon as you can. Tomorrow, better still tonight."

"Why?"

"This place isn't safe not for you. It's haunted."

"Of course It's haunted," said Jonathan. "You're here."

"I don't mean haunted by me," said Dave fiercely. "I mean really haunted, by one of those earth-bound spirits I told you about — that possessed you this afternoon. Something really powerful – and it's coming for you."

Jonathan drew a deep breath. "So what do I do?"

"Stay awake, mate. Sit up all night. And if it does appear, don't go with it. I only just got you back twice today and the pull's much stronger now. If you get trapped on the Other Side . . . "

Jonathan shuddered. "I know. I'll be a ghost like you. A ghost from the future."

Suddenly the candle blew out and the door flew open.

A young man in flying clothes stood in the doorway. It was one of the young men Jonathan had seen at the airfield that afternoon, the one who'd stared at him.

The figure beckoned.

"No," whispered Dave. "Don't go. Remember what I told you."

Jonathan felt not only a pull but a sort of desperate appeal coming from the figure in the doorway. "I've got to go with him, Dave. He needs help. Might as well get it over with."

"No!" shouted Dave.

Ignoring him, Jonathan lay back and closed his eyes. Immediately he felt himself drawn away . . .

Suddenly he was back on the airfield, scrambling desperately to reach his plane.

This time he let himself be swept forward with the others.

"Scramble! Scramble! Scramble!" squawked the tannoy. "Airfield under attack." Jonathan pounded across the grass and climbed into the cockpit of his Spitfire.

The corporal mechanic was standing by, and helped to strap him in. He pulled down the transparent canopy, and made a rapid instrument check. With automatic skill his hands moved over the controls and the Merlin engines coughed into life.

He waved to the corporal who jumped off the wing and pulled the chocks from under the wheels. Jonathan, or rather the Spitfire pilot Jonathan had become, opened the throttle and the plane jolted across the grass and seemed to leap into the sky.

As always it swung a little on take-off, but he soon had it trimmed. Came off the ground pretty sharpish, the old Spitfire, he thought.

And you could see all around you too, thanks to the transparent canopy. He checked the weaponry, eight Browning machine-guns, four housed in each wing . . .

Almost immediately, the machine-guns came into use.

The enemy were up in force, and he found himself above a Dornier bomber, one of those attacking the field. Screaming down he raked it again and again with machine-gun fire. The Dornier staggered, sending out streams of smoke, but it didn't go down. Built like flying tanks, those Dorniers . . .

Still it was crippled and had to turn for home.

Immediately he was engaged with one of the Messerschmidt BF 109's that formed the bomber escort.

Switching on the reflector sight and turning the safety catch back to 'fire' position he opened the throttle and sped straight towards the enemy. He opened fire at almost point-blank range, and a spray of oil on his windscreen showed him the Messerschmidt was hit.

Glancing down, he saw it spinning towards the ground giving out a thick trail of smoke.

All around the air seemed full of planes, the attacking bombers and their Messerschmidt fighter escorts. The bombers of course were the main target, but each bomber was protected by fighters.

With a savage burst of fire he blew the canopy from an attacking Messerschmidt, and as he shot by he saw the white canopy of its pilot's parachute drifting towards the ground.

Swooping up on another enemy fighter from below he blew up the tail unit with an accurate burst of fire.

Suddenly he became aware of an enemy fighter on his tail. He sideslipped to port and then to starboard, but the fighter still hung on.

He flicked over into a stall-turn, raking the enemy with his machine-guns as the Messerschmidt flashed by sideways-on, presenting an unmissable target.

The Messerschmidt burst into flames and went down in a flat spin, exploding as it hit the ground.

And so the afternoon went on as the Spitfires made darting attacks at the lumbering bombers, and fought savage one-to-one battles with their fighter escorts . . .

His final battle came just as the day was ending.

He spotted another BF 109, just coming out of its turn a few thousand yards ahead. The German saw him at the same time and spun towards him, attacking head on.

Peering through his reflector sight he opened fire, and the Messerschmidt fired at the same time. He could feel the bullets thudding into the Spitfire and the BF 109 was so close it looked as if they must crash. At the last minute he looped first under and then up and over the Messerschmidt, diving down out of the setting sun and raking the enemy from above.

The Messerschmidt went into a spin, spiralling downwards streaming smoke. A numbness in his side and the faltering in his engine told him that both he and his Spitfire were badly damaged.

In the failing light, he struggled to regain the airfield. The engines cut out and the Spitfire glided silently downwards . . .

Both the light and his own sight were failing now, and he was flying into a silvery haze.

There below him was a long smooth stretch of grass. Was it his field, or some other? No matter, it was the perfect spot for an emergency landing . . .

He made a final effort and brought ˙the

plane into land.

It was only as his wheels were about to touch down that he realised that the ground below wasn't ground at all . . .

* * *

Jonathan was himself again, but that self was lost, floating in misty nothingness.

He shuddered, remembering Dave's warnings. Was he trapped here forever, doomed to float in this limbo, while his real body withered and died . . . ?

He was gripped by a sensation of overpowering terror. He felt literally paralysed by fear.

Suddenly he saw a glowing figure just ahead.

A tall young man in pilot's uniform. The figure beckoned, and Jonathan followed . . .

CHAPTER FIVE

Homecoming

Jonathan awoke.

Someone was shaking his shoulder.

Not his mum, not Dave . . .

He opened his eyes and saw Great-Aunt Caroline glaring indignantly down at him. "I know you are on holiday, young man, but I really felt I had to wake you. It's past mid-day."

Jonathan blinked. "Sorry, I've had rather a tiring night. I'll get up now."

"So I should hope."

As the old lady stomped off a frantic Dave materialised. "You're back! I've been searching for you, but I couldn't find you.

How did you manage it?"

"*He* brought me back, Dave, the pilot. I know what he wants me to do now."

"What is it?"

Jonathan shook his head. "Not yet. If my theory's right you'll see in good time, and so will everyone else." He jumped out of bed. "I need a bit more information before I'm completely sure. And I know just the man to give it to me . . ."

*   *   *

The Wingco was sitting in front of the pub with his pint when Jonathan pedalled up.

He seemed delighted to see him. "Come for another ear-bashing, my lad? You're a glutton for punishment, you are. Still, they were glorious days, you know. We stood alone, defying the Nazi hordes!"

Dave appeared and gave a cheer, and Jonathan said hurriedly, "And you were here throughout the Battle of Britain, at the airfield?"

"Yes, indeed. Only a small field, mind, but we did our bit. I could tell you some tales . . ."

And so he did, going on for quite a while.

When the flow of stories looked like tailing off, Jonathan said, "I'm interested in one particular pilot actually. I don't know if you knew him."

"Knew 'em all," said the Wingco. "What was his name?"

"That's the problem, I don't know. I can tell you what he looked like, tall, thin-faced, dark eyes. I don't think he was with you very long. He probably got shot down soon after he arrived."

"So did quite a few of them," said the Wingco sadly. "We were using pilots without proper experience towards the end, all we'd got. Lads fresh out of flying school, and a cutdown course at that. Quite a few didn't last very long."

Suddenly Jonathan remembered going back in time to the crowded bar. "A bitter for Tom," the pilot had said.

"I can tell you his first name – Tom. He used to drink bitter."

The Wingco gazed into space as if picturing long-vanished faces. Then he pounded his fist on the table. "Tom Brown!"

Just the sort of nice ordinary name he'd choose, thought Jonathan. Out loud he said, "That sounds like the one. What happened to him?"

"Poor old Tom Brown," said the Wingco sadly. "Came to us straight from flying school in Canada – a lot of our pilots trained over there. Good looking young devil, liked a drink and a laugh . . ."

Jonathan was more and more certain he'd got the right man. "What happened?" he asked again.

"He was with us three days. Then he vanished. Missing in action."

"How did it happen?"

"It was the day they decided to hit our airfield. Came over just as we were ready to take off. Heck of a dogfight, went on all day. Somewhere in the middle of it all, young Tom Brown vanished. Someone said they'd seen him down a Messerschmidt near the end of the day, but after that he just disappeared. Radar was out, communications out, anything could have happened. Went down in the drink, most likely."

Perhaps, thought Jonathan. Or perhaps . . .

He jumped up. "Thanks a lot for the talk, sir. Now there's someone I've got to see." He ran into the inn and bumped into Jack Potter coming down the stairs. "The very man," said Jonathan breathlessly. "Now listen, I may be able to get Great-Aunt Caroline interested. Suppose I persuade her to talk to you, and maybe even make some kind of deal."

Jack Potter gave him a slap on the back that nearly knocked him over.

"That would be terrific!"

"But if she does, you've got to promise to do something."

"Like what?"

Jonathan told him.

Jack Potter said, "But we'd have had to do that anyway. The foundations for the harbour . . . "

"I know," said Jonathan. "I just want you to do it sooner rather than later."

They talked for a while longer, then Jack said, "Okay! You get the old dear to sign on the dotted line, and it's a deal."

As Jonathan pedalled furiously back to the house, he heard Dave's voice in his ear. "Look, what do you think you're up to, mate?"

"You'll see," said Jonathan. "If I can only persuade Great-Aunt Caroline, you'll all see."

"See what?"

"The answer to a mystery – nearly fifty years old . . . "

* * *

Jonathan's whole scheme nearly came a cropper over Great-Aunt Caroline.

"Certainly not!" said the old lady furiously. "I've already told you, I won't hear of it. My responsibility is to the village."

"Seems to me your responsibility is to

bring the place to life, not sit by and watch it die slowly. And they're offering a wonderful deal . . . A seat on the board for you, and a handsome salary. You'd have final say on all the designs . . . "

Jonathan had to talk himself hoarse before the old lady would grudgingly consent to at least meet and talk with the developers.

And of course, it didn't help at all that he couldn't possibly tell her the real reason why he was so keen for the deal to go through . . .

* * *

It was dawn, the lowest of low tide a couple of days later. Jonathan, Jack Potter and Freddie Purbright and Great-Aunt Caroline were all standing on the sea wall between the sea and the lagoon, just close to the airfield. The Wingco was there as well, and so was Dave, although no-one but Jonathan could see him.

It had taken a lot of talk and negotiation and deal-making to get them all here, and Jonathan only hoped it was going to be worth it.

"It's basically a simple enough process," Jack Potter was saying. "We blow out a chunk of sea wall at low tide, and the lagoon drains out onto the sands. We reckon that'll take less than an hour. That gives us a couple of hours to repair the damage so the sea can't flood back in. Everyone ready?"

No one said they weren't so Jack Potter waved a signal to a hard-hatted figure some way along the wall.

The man waved back, bent over a black box and seconds later there was a *crump* sound and a spurt of earth and sand from a point in the sea wall half-way between him and them.

"How disappointing," said Great-Aunt Caroline. "I was expecting something far more spectacular."

"We want to breach the sea wall, not blow it up," said Jack Potter. "Water pressure will do most of the work for us."

For a time it seemed nothing was happening.

Then they saw lagoon water flooding out over the sands, and slowly the water level in the lagoon started to fall.

As it fell, a shape began to appear from

beneath the water.

First the tail, then part of the fuselage, then a wing-tip . . .

They watched in amazement as the shape of the complete plane was finally revealed. "What on earth . . . " whispered Great-Aunt Caroline. "What is it?"

"It's the last Spitfire," said Jonathan. "Flown by your vanished nephew, Tristram Boone."

*　　*　　*

"You see he must have listened to you after all," said Jonathan. "Instead of going to America he stayed in Canada and enlisted in a flying school under the name of Tom Brown."

They were all sitting in the private parlour of the inn, drinking coffee supplied by the astonished landlady.

"Then, of course, he got posted to this airfield, right next to your house."

Great-Aunt Caroline was still dazed. "But why didn't he come and see me?"

"I expect he would have," said Jonathan.

"He'd only been there a few days, remember. Maybe he wanted to do something to make you proud of him before he turned up."

"Well, he certainly did that," said the old lady softly.

The Wingco said, "And he was trying to get back to base, probably wounded with his plane damaged and he made it just as far as the lagoon."

Jack Potter shook his head. "Amazing. How did you work all this out, young fellow?"

"Oh, luck and guesswork," said Jonathan vaguely.

After all, there was no way he could tell them the truth.

Great-Aunt Caroline said sadly, "And now I can have his portrait painted at last — and hang it in the gallery with my other dead heroes."

*   *   *

It wasn't until very much later that Jonathan could talk about what had really happened. And, of course, the only one he could talk to was Dave.

They sat together on a deserted stretch of the sea wall, watching the crowd gathering round the Spitfire on the lagoon bed. Already the police had roped the plane off, and the pilot's body had been taken away. Eventually Tristram Boone's body would lie in the local churchyard beside his ancestors, and, Jonathan hoped, his spirit would finally be at rest.

"I'm still not sure how I got drawn in to all this," he said.

Dave said importantly, "I reckon it was because of me."

"Why you?"

"Well poor old Tristram couldn't get through to the old girl, see. She's the sort that won't believe in ghosts and never sees them.

But when you and I met, I reckon that somehow he managed to get to know about you."

"On the ghosts' grapevine, you mean?"

"I am talking about the astral plane, mate," said Dave with dignity. "Don't mock. Anyway, he was able to plant the idea of sending for you in the old girl's mind when she was asleep. Then when you turned up, he used you to get the truth brought to light. You did a good job there, mate."

"So I've got you to thank, have I?" said Jonathan. "As if it isn't bad enough to get haunted once, I get haunted twice."

Dave gave him a reproachful look. "Come off it mate, you ought to be grateful! How many kids can say they've flown a Spitfire in the Battle of Britain?"

"How many people can I tell about it?" asked Jonathan.

"I don't know," said Dave. "Some people are never satisfied."

"Come on," said Jonathan. "Let's take a closer look at my plane."